DER[EK THE]

DEPRESSED VIKING

in...

Kidnapped by Ice Maidens

Extremely unpleasant Ice

Rough Ice

Tough Ice

Nasty Ice

KEITH BRUMPTON

 ORCHARD BOOKS

OTHER BOOKS BY KEITH BRUMPTON
(and remember, each book bought goes towards
a Torquay United season ticket)

Dinosaur World Cup
A Dinosaur's Book of Dinosaurs
Ig and Tig's Trip to Earth
The Mystery of the Missing Moggy
The Mystery of the Dog with 1,000 Disguises
The Mystery of the Great Sheepdog Swindle
The Mystery of the Dachshund Diamonds
· DEREK BOOKS ·
The Dragon from the Black Lagoon
Nice throne, Shame about the Crown
Who'd be a Viking?

To find out more about Keith Brumpton's books,
visit his website at:
http://www.okukbooks.com/kbrumpton/

Contents

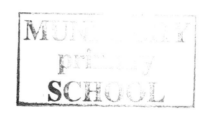

All characters in this book are
entirely fictitious, except for the
character of Sven Forkbeard, who is
based on Mr. M. Phelps of 63,
Dothelocomotion Road, York.
Anyone interested in further exploring
the Viking period should build themselves
a time machine.
The Author would like to thank the following:
The Happy Valley Pet-shop (biscuits)
The Oslo Viking Society (advice on beards)
Dr. Natasha Trabant (samples of Viking D.N.A)

ORCHARD BOOKS
96 Leonard Street, London EC2A 4RH
Orchard Books Australia
14 Mars Road, Lane Cove, NSW 2066
First published in Great Britain 1998
First paperback publication 1999
Copyright © Keith Brumpton 1998
The right of Keith Brumpton to be identified as the Author and
Illustrator of this Work has been asserted by him in accordance
with the Copyright, Designs and Patents Act, 1988.
A CIP catalogue record for this book is available from the
British Library.
1 86039 358 6 (hardback)
1 86039 602 X (paperback)
Printed in Great Britain

Chapter One: Coward's End.

Things had not been going well for Derek
the Depressed Viking.

It had all started a few months back,
when he'd been so nervous during battle that
his teeth had chattered and his knees had
knocked together like two conkers on a
windy night. To make matters worse, he'd
only been scuffling with a couple of monks.
Now, if there's one thing the Vikings didn't
like, it was a coward.

Some other things Vikings didn't like:

1. Monks:

2. Shaving:

3. Wolves:

(Some of them didn't like Port Vale very much either.)

Olaf Dednafffellur was Derek's sworn enemy, and he took great pleasure in reporting the knee-knocking business to Chief Harald.

"...Two, he refused to go up the mast during a thunderstorm... And three, his teeth were chattering all through the battle... He was only taking on a couple of monks from Abbey-tat*!"

"He's lucky he's still got teeth," mumbled the Chief. "I lost mine while

---

* Famous local superstore. See 'Nice Throne, Shame about the Crown'.

wrestling with a giant bear."

The Chief summoned Derek to explain his cowardly behaviour.

Our hero's cheeks turned bright red and he struggled to think of a good excuse...

"It was a cold day, Chief, and I'd forgotten my vest."

Under Viking law, the penalty for

cowardice was death. This was one penalty Derek wouldn't mind missing. Viking executions could be very nasty affairs indeed. The Chief thought for a moment, and then rose to give his verdict...

Was Derek for the chop? Would his head and shoulders soon be heading in opposite directions? What was the Chief's decision??!

Chapter Two: Not More Pie, Please!

SURPRISE
VERDICT IN
D. DEREK
COWARDICE
TRIAL

·THE EVENING RUNES·

As it turned out, the Chief decided not to execute Derek after all. His daughter, Anka, (who quite liked Derek) pleaded for his life to be spared, and since the Chief didn't like upsetting her, he announced a different punishment...

You will become my new food taster.

11

Derek felt depressed. Not as depressed as he would have done if he'd been sentenced to death, but still quite depressed.

Everyone knew that being the Chief's food taster was a risky job. People were always trying to kill the Chief, hoping to make themselves chief. And one of their favourite methods was to try to poison his food. That's why Chief Harald always employed someone to taste his food first... If the food taster was OK, then so was the food. If the food taster fell to the floor writhing in agony, then the chief would eat out...

A Big Elk with fries to go...

↑ ex-food taster

So it was that Derek found himself seated at the Chief's table, about to try his fifth reindeer pie. Not only was his new job very risky, he was also putting on quite a bit of weight.

Still, at least it was better than having to face his mother's cooking, and only slightly riskier.

There was another bonus too. As the Chief's official food taster, he had to be close by on all occasions, so he got to eat and sleep in the Chief's luxury hut. (It had a roof and some straw.)

This made the evenings very comfortable. Much better than his normal spot next to the pig sty. There was a warm fire all evening, a cosy bed of straw, and even better, he didn't have to listen to his mother telling him stories of brave deeds performed by his ancestors...

And then your grandfather raised his sword again and drew up his shield and... Derek, I'm not boring you, am I?

Of course not, mum...

★   ★   ★

Derek was snug in his straw. He closed his eyes and began to doze. The whole village lay still and calm. Except, that is, for a mysterious group of tall, heavily armoured figures who were crouched outside the Chief's hut... The moonlight glinted off their pointy helmets and revealed sharp, silvery axes and deadly, gleaming swords...

The Chief's hut was about to be attacked, and Derek was in there, sound asleep. Would he wake in time? Would the reindeer pie slow him down as he tried to run away?

The mysterious figures sneaked inside the hut and still no one stirred...

Chapter Three: One of our Vikings is Missing.

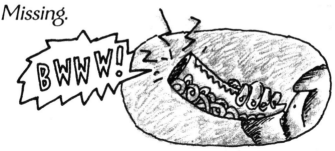

It was Erik Raven's-nose who first raised the alarm. Where did he raise it to? Don't ask me.

He blew his horn, loud and hard, like an angry motorist caught in holiday traffic.

"To arms! To arms!"

And fast as a bolt of Thor's lightning, the warriors of Upper Elkshead gathered their axes, swords, shields, and those metal balls with spikes on them which don't seem to have a name, and rushed to the Chief's hut to see what was happening.

Derek, meanwhile, was many leagues hence. A very long way off in other words. He was being dragged along, arms and legs tied together, by two of the tallest women he'd ever seen. There were more women up ahead, equally tall, and carrying spears.

Derek couldn't remember how he came to be in this situation. He'd been sound asleep, dreaming of the princess Anka, when suddenly he'd heard voices, felt someone grab a hold of him, and then...nothing. These women must have knocked him out and made him their prisoner. But who were they, and why had they done this to him?

Wouldn't you like to know?!

*   *   *

Frank the seagull perched himself on top of the Chief's hut and listened to the commotion below. From what he could hear, it seemed someone had attacked during the night and tried to take the Chief prisoner. Luckily, they'd made a mistake and taken the wrong Viking. Chief Harald was alive and well and in a very bad mood. But who had dared to attack the village and who was the unfortunate Viking they'd kidnapped?

19

Frank quickly guessed. His friend, Derek, had been sleeping in the Chief's hut and it was he who'd got nabbed by mistake! As to the identity of the kidnappers, there was no doubt about it, they were the Ice Maidens. A tribe of very tall, very blood-thirsty fighting women from a place called Knutsfjord. They were stronger than most men, bitter enemies of the Vikings, and this was just their style. There was a saying in Upper Elkshead:

The Princess Anka recognised Frank the seagull, and knew him to be a good friend of Derek's.

"This is bad news indeed. Those Ice Maidens are a mean bunch. If they find out Derek isn't the real chief he's in big trouble."

"You mean they'd do him in?"

"He's always frightened out of his wits."

"That's true, but you know what I mean. He really *is* in trouble this time."

Chapter Four: A Little Light Dusting.

It was early evening, the sun was setting behind the mountains, and Derek had begun to feel quite comfortable in his new surroundings. Unaware of the fearsome reputation of his kidnappers, our weary hero was stretched out on some straw, wondering if things might not have turned out for the best after all.

It's better than my room at home!

True, he had been kidnapped, but by a tribe of women, so at least there would be no more fighting. Derek began to imagine himself in a new life... Doing a bit of gardening, putting up the odd fence, helping the women with their shopping. A smile began to form on his face. The first one for quite a while.

"No more swords and axes... It'll be needle and thread, night classes, and a spot of baby-sitting."

Suddenly a shadow fell across Derek. A very large shadow. He looked up to see a rather formidable woman, dressed in full battle-dress and carrying a long and deadly looking sword.

"On your feet," she snarled, with an accent Derek didn't recognise. "My name is Valkerie Halla, but my enemies call me Val."

Val... Halla... the name seems familiar. *

* There is a joke here...if you know your Viking mythology.

"...It was my idea to kidnap you and bring you here. We have sent a ransom note to your village. They will pay many gold pieces for the safe return of a famous warrior such as yourself...Chief Harald Hafnomörssy."

The smile had now vanished from Derek's face and had packed its bags ready for a long holiday.

There has been an awful mistake here, thought Derek. They think I'm Chief Harald. And they want a ransom for my return. But no one at Upper Elkshead would pay a penny to get me back. Except the Princess Anka and she's too young to have any loot.

"You don't look well," continued Val Halla. "Perhaps you need some exercise?"

Derek felt a little colour return to his cheeks. "I like music and dancing."

For some reason Val Halla laughed. A loud and cruel laugh. And it seemed to Derek that her laugh travelled out from the hut, up into the mountains and echoed round and round in the chill night air. It sent a shiver down his spine and left a tingle in his tibia. What was this mysterious Parade of Spears?

Chapter Five: The Mysterious Parade of Spears.

Derek had what the Vikings would call 'a good seat'. We probably wouldn't agree, because it was only a piece of icy-cold rock which was rapidly chilling his bottom. But from where he was seated he could have a very good view of the Parade of Spears, whatever that was.

As he took his place he tried not to look around too much, but he couldn't help but notice that the women in this particular village were taller than any he'd ever seen before. And they were all dressed in full armour. Perhaps it was some sort of festival. But when were the local men returning?

A large girl with her hair in ginger plaits sat down next to him and Derek had to squeeze along a bit.

"Looking forward to the show?" she asked.

"Very much so," replied Derek, shyly. "Are there any comedy routines?"

The ginger-haired girl smiled a cruel smile. "You are a brave man, to sit here among the Ice Maidens of Knutsfjord and to laugh and joke as you do."

The rusty cogs of Derek's memory were slowly beginning to turn. Something told him this Parade of Spears might not be some sort of cheery version of *Riverdance* after all...

To the beating of a loud, booming drum, the Parade began...

Sixty Ice Maidens dressed in gleaming chain-mail strode forward, each carrying a shield and a large, extremely large in fact, pointed spear. They stamped their spears on the ground in time to the beating of the drum. And as they stamped they sang:

At the end of the song, they suddenly turned and threw their swords towards Derek. A whole hail of them landed at his feet with a whistle and thud.

The girl next to Derek laughed and clapped her hands. "That's the nearest we get to comedy."

Glad I wasn't in the front row!

Derek mopped his brow. Forgetting that his mother had sewn his name onto his handkerchief. The ginger-haired girl, whose name was Bjork (Bjork Minster, if you'd like to write to her) spotted the writing on Derek's handkerchief and asked if she could borrow it.

"*'Property of Derek Drodnodrott'*," she read, slowly.

"Thanks."

Derek then realised his mistake. "Derek is my, er, nickname... I never liked the name Harald...!"

But it was too late and too unconvincing. Word spread quickly among the Ice Maidens, and before long had reached the ears of the formidable Val Halla herself. She strode over to Derek like a bear with a sore head. And toothache.

"So!!! You're not Chief Harald... You're a nobody! Just one of his bodyguards."

Well, I...

You look like a fighting man. I should have guessed you were the BRAWN and not the brains...

I'm the jelly actually.

I, er...

What's your name? I know some of Harald's top boys.

Derek...

"Derek? Derek what? Derek the Daring? Derek the Deadly?"

"Derek the Depressed."

"Never heard of you. But you'll do."

"Do?"

"Yes, for some time now the Ladies First Team has needed someone to coach them. You, a chief's bodyguard, will give us all the tactics and techniques we need...the axe, the broadsword, how to scale a cliff, fight at sea, wrestle..."

Derek felt this wasn't the time to disappoint Valkerie Halla. He thought about offering to start by repairing a few fences or helping with the washing up, but decided against it. The Parade of Spears had almost ended. The Ice Maidens were taking part in a mock battle. Actually, it looked pretty rough for a mock battle.

Derek fidgeted on his rocky seat. Val Halla hadn't finished with him yet.

"I should add that once you've finished training my troops, we shall see how much ransom Upper Elkshead offers for you. If it's less than forty pieces of gold, then we shall hurl you off Pointy Rock Point."

Derek wasn't familiar with this particular spot, but from the name, it didn't seem a very promising place to be hurled from. And hurled he would be, because there was no way anyone in Upper Elkshead would cough up four pieces of gold, let alone forty!

Pointy Rock Point.
How ever had it got its name?

Chapter Six: A Handsome Ransom.

Chief Harald was so busy opening his mail, he didn't even notice the seagull perched at the far end of the hut.

DEAR CHIEF HARALD,

Now listen to this if you know what's good for you. We have got one of your boys here. We've got him safely under lock and key.

He's one of your bodyguards. Calls himself DEREK.

DEREK the Depresser... One mean fighting machine. If you want him back in one piece, then send a messenger with 40 pieces of gold to your old friends, the ICE GIRLS...

Yours threateningly,
The Ice Maidens of Knutsfjord

The chief folded the parchment for a moment. "So they've got poor Derek."

With friends like the Chief, who needs enemies?

Soon word had spread all round the village of Derek's plight. The Princess Anka started a fund to raise money for Derek's return, but the response was slow...

Frank asked the Princess how much she'd managed to raise so far.

"Er...nothing. But his mother has promised to try and chip in if anyone else does."

Frank cocked his head to one side. "There's nothing else for it, I'm going to have to try and find him. I didn't want to risk it, because I don't know those skies very well, but..."

The Princess wished him luck and said she'd keep on trying to raise the forty gold pieces.

There was another golden sunset as Frank the seagull took off on his mission of mercy. His destination was Knutsfjord, his beak full of fish for the journey.

Chapter Seven: One Step from Pointy Rock Point.

It was very early in the morning. Derek knew this because his legs were still asleep and he didn't even feel hungry enough to eat breakfast. Not that it looked particularly appetising anyway...

Even so, Derek tried to make the meal last as long as possible because he knew it might be his last. In a few minutes' time he was due to meet the Ice Maiden warriors in order to teach them how to improve their one-to-one sword-fighting skills. Derek's main tactic in such situations was to run away very quickly, but he didn't think this would impress the Ice Girls.

Val Halla appeared in the doorway, blocking out the sun for a moment.

"Ever ready. That's my motto," mumbled Derek, taking a last mouthful of hare soup. "Ever ready for a sharp exit."

The Ice Maidens had assembled in a grassy field near to the water's edge. Derek couldn't help wondering whether Pointy Rock Point was close by.

"What skills will you teach us first?" asked a fierce-looking lady with several teeth missing. Derek was in a tight corner.

"Before we do any actual fighting, it's very important that we warm up properly. I'd like to start with a few light exercises."

"There's no time to do warm-ups before going into battle!" spluttered Valkerie Halla, but Derek ignored her.

"Gently now, hands on hips, begin circling. Yes, big circles, reach up now and try to touch the sky, mind you don't cut yourselves on your swords...then breathe in, nice big breaths..."

So far so good, thought Derek to himself. But how long can I keep them doing warm-up exercises?

* * *

Frank the seagull had make good progress, but his wings were aching. He hadn't eaten for hours and the wind was against him. It was a salty, sea-spray sort of a wind, so he knew he was still on course. But how long would it take to reach the land of the Ice Maidens? And would Derek still be alive to be rescued? Frank flapped harder and found a warm air current he could glide on for a while... Down below he could see a white beach. Was this Knutsfjord?

Derek felt the chains around his ankles, and felt depressed. So the Ice Maidens hadn't been impressed by his fighting skills, but they hadn't exactly given him much of a chance. Even Manchester City managers lasted longer than half an hour. That was all they'd given Derek before it became clear he knew less about sword-fighting than a monk from the Holy Island Flower-Arranging Society.

Nothing worse than a sword stuck in the scabbard...

← desperate tug

Val Halla gave the order for Derek to be seized and led away to a spot where he could watch the Ice Maidens continue their training. Not that they looked as if they needed much training.

They'd be a match for anyone, thought Derek to himself. Even Chief Harald, Sven and the boys back home...

Val Halla called out to her muscular maidens.

"Tomorrow we'll sail for Upper Elkshead. And this time, now we know they're so weak and feeble, we won't take a hostage, we'll take out the whole village."

Spears were raised. Feet were stamped. Blond pigtails swung menacingly. Derek's day seemed to be getting worse by the minute, a bit like being at school really. All he needed now was for someone to mention Pointy Rock Point.

Bring the prisoner to Pointy Rock Point!

Bingo!

Chapter Eight: Fancy a Drop?

Up until now, Derek had always enjoyed a walk in the country. But this particular trip wasn't proving very enjoyable. Perhaps it was the chains around his wrists, or the occasional prod from a spear, or possibly the fact that Pointy Rock Point didn't look like the sort of place to hold a picnic.

A tall grey cliff, ending in a dramatic ice-cream cone shaped peak now appeared before our luckless hero.

"Don't you fancy having a man around the place?" he asked one of the Ice Maidens, in a last attempt to talk his way to freedom.

Derek asked what they were going to do to him. He was pretty sure they'd mention hurling him into the sea, but he just wanted to be sure.

"You'll be left on the top of the cliff. It's so narrow that as soon as your legs weaken you'll fall into the sea. And even if you don't fall, the tide will come in and you'll drown. Any more questions?"

Derek was too worried to think of any. He'd always known a Viking's life was tough, but this was the toughest corner he'd ever been in. Tougher than a corner of his mother's home-baked bread.

The Ice Maidens' spears pointed the way, as Derek continued alone up the very narrow ledge which led to the top of Pointy Rock Point.

He noticed a human skull and one or two bones.

Whilst the women stood and laughed, Derek was blindfolded. One false move and he'd fall to his death. Blindfolded, he stood no chance of escaping back down the right route.

Chapter Nine: Derek can't see the Point.

The wind off the sea was icy and Derek's nose was getting cold. He was also worried about falling to his death at any moment. He thought about the Princess Anka and wondered if, one peaceful summer's night, when they'd been out walking together...

"Deggsie..."
"Princess?"
"No, you fool, it's me, Frank."

"Frank?" Derek's heart quickened, like an Ethiopian marathon runner in the final straight. "Is it really you?"

"Of course it's me," squawked the loyal seagull. "Who else is going to be hanging round a place like this? Now, don't move until I tell you to."

"Yes, I can see that." Frank had already worked out that the only way to save Derek was to guide him back down the ledge, to a point of safety. The problem being that Derek would be blindfolded.

He told Derek to follow his directions, and to concentrate very hard. "And I hope you know your left from your right."

"Am I safe?" Derek asked, his knees still trembling.

"Well, you're off Pointy Rock Point, but we still have to get rid of that blindfold... Remember, we're still in Ice Maiden territory."

"Mmm. How could I forget?" Normally, Derek would have run away, but he couldn't do that while he was still unsighted.

"Couldn't you get this blindfold off?"

"Sorry, we seagulls aren't much good at knots. We'll have to walk along the coast and hope we meet someone friendly."

Derek shrugged his shoulders. He'd been a Viking twenty-eight years and in all that time he'd only met one friendly person. Plus a co-operative seagull.

It was then that he remembered the Ice Maidens and their plan to attack Upper Elkshead. Derek explained the plot to Frank, who decided they'd better take a short-cut through the woods instead.

"The Ice Maidens will travel in their longboat. But moving quickly in a straight line through the forest we can beat them to it!"

It seemed a good plan, though Derek wished he could see where he was going...

Chapter Ten: The Last Chapter before Chapter Eleven.*

Guided by Frank, exhausted and hungry, Derek finally stumbled into his home village just as the sun was beginning to rise. He'd been walking for thirteen hours and had a blister.

"Raise the alarm, the Ice Maidens are about to attack!" he called out, dramatically.

It took a while for Derek's eyes to get adjusted to the light. Everything was shimmery and vague.

"Sorry, Olaf, my eyes were a bit funny after wearing the blindfold for so long. Did you raise the alarm?"

"No. No need to wake anyone yet. I need more proof."

"But I heard their plans myself!"

Frank the seagull decided to take matters into his own webbed feet and uttered a piercing shriek.

The sound woke half the village, and one by one they emerged, amazed to see Derek back safe and sound. And even more amazed when they heard of his daring escape. Chief Harald welcomed him like a long-lost son, and listened with concern to the story of the Ice Maidens and their plan to attack the village.

Derek had hoped he might be given the day off as a reward for good behaviour, but no such luck. He had to take part in the battle just like everyone else.

"Helmet?"

"Yes, Mum."

"Axe?"

"Yes, Mum."

"Clean handkerchief?"

"Yes!"

"DWWWWOOO!"

motherly shove

A long horn call signalled the beginning of the battle. The Ice Maidens had arrived and were swarming ashore from their longboat. Derek recognised Val Halla in her fearsome head-dress, and one or two other women he'd fought with during the training sessions.

Frank the seagull swooped low to give a last piece of advice.

"Keep your shield out in front and don't pick on anyone taller than yourself."

Easier said than done. These are big girls!

The battle raged. Derek found himself opposite Val Halla herself. He had a point to prove. Unfortunately she had a point too...on the end of her spear. But Derek had learned a trick or two whilst watching the Ice Maidens' training sessions, and to his surprise he seemed to be coping quite well.

"How did you escape from Pointy Rock Point?" asked Val Halla, as they paused for breath.

"My mum said it's rude to talk during battles," replied Derek, and waved his axe menacingly.

The battle was long and hard. Many spears were snapped. But gradually, with home advantage and seeing Deggsie fighting like a man possessed, the Vikings of Upper Elkshead took heart, and by sundown the Ice Maidens were a broken force. Val Halla herself gave the signal to retreat.

Within minutes, they'd all fled back to their longboat and begun the long journey back to Knutsfjord. Chief Harald gathered everyone outside his hut.

"Well done, men! And especially to Derek Drodnodrott, who has proved himself a warrior of the highest order. Derek, henceforth you will no longer be my food taster. That honour passes to... Olaf Dednafffellur."

That night, after a magnificent banquet and some marvellous stories told by the chief himself, Derek and Anka went for a walk along the beach. The moon was full, the stars were bright, the waves lapped on the shore.

Anka handed Derek a note. "It's from your mum."

"Dear Derek," it read.

"Sorry I won't be here when you get back. I've decided to run off and become an Ice Maiden. You know I always liked a good scrap. It'll be a good chance for me to travel, see the world and throw my weight around a bit. Your dinner's in the oven.

Saw your last fight. You were great.

Thor be with you,
Mum."

"Good news?" asked the Princess.

"I think it probably is," replied Derek, after a while. "But it looks like I'll be cooking my own tea from now on!"

"You could always apply for your old job as food taster."

"Er, no thanks."

And as they looked up they saw thousands of stars.

A last squawk from Frankie...

OK, guys and gulls, so that's it for another adventure. Once again we've seen that you don't have to be a tough guy or a genius to get by in life. All you need is a little luck, a kind heart, and a helpful gull-friend. Stay runed until the next time...

And keep your shields up!